# Conkers

First published in 2016 in Great Britain by
Barrington Stoke Ltd, 18 Walker Street, Edinburgh, EH3 7LP

www.barringtonstoke.co.uk

Text © 2016 Georgia Byng
Illustrations © 2016 Gary Blythe

A CIP catalogue record for this book is available from the British
Library upon request

ISBN: 978-1-78112-569-4

Printed in China by Leo

# GEORGIA BYNG

# The Girl with No Nose

### WITH ILLUSTRATIONS BY
# GARY BLYTHE

Conkers

*For my dear Christopher – lighthouse, beacon.*
*Thank you.*

# CONTENTS

# CHAPTER 1

# Times of Change

Alice Peasbody lived in Victorian times.

Let me remind you. These were times when chimney sweeps sent small children up chimneys. And, if they didn't clean them quick enough, the sweeps would light a fire underneath them.

These were times when teachers beat left-handed children until they learned to write with their right hands.

These were times when women weren't allowed to vote.

These were times when circus audiences came to laugh at 'freaks' – at the man with the elephant face, or at the lady who was so fat she couldn't stand, or at the Siamese twins whose bodies were joined at the hip.

These were times when there were gallows in every city and for entertainment on a Saturday people liked to watch a criminal being hung by the neck until he or she were dead.

Luckily, these Victorian times were also times of change. Change for the good can happen when good people shine a light on what is bad.  Alice Peasbody was one of these good people – one of these bright lights – although for a long time she didn't know it.

# CHAPTER 2
## Pancake Face

Alice Peasbody had two names. Alice Peasbody, and a nickname that other children gave her – Pancake Face.

People called her Pancake Face because she didn't have a nose.

When she was born, her mother saw the baby Alice and thought she was dreaming. "WHERE'S HER NOSE?" she screamed.

Her father stared accusingly at the midwife.
The midwife looked about on the floor, as if worried
for a moment that Alice's nose had actually dropped
off.

But then Alice burped and her parents' hearts
melted.  And they loved her completely, even though

they knew that, in lots of people's eyes, Alice was not complete.

When Alice's mother took her out, people would peer into the pram, thinking that Alice was a broken doll. When Alice moved, they'd gasp and jump back in horror with a cry, or even a horrible exclamation like, "You ought to have that thing put down, Missis." Or, "Uuuurgh, that's a *monster*, that is." Some would even laugh and blurt out, "You gotta be jokin'." The kinder people would say, "Oh my word," or, "Bless it."

Without a nose, Alice was to most people a creature more than a person.

When Alice went to school and the other children saw her, they whispered that she had a disease that made your nose fall off. They said that Alice's ears would fall off next. They teased Alice by holding mouldy cheese and rotten fish under her no-nose. Alice pretended she could smell the cheese and fish, even though she absolutely couldn't. She wanted to be normal as possible.

"I do smell," she insisted. "It's only my nose that I'm missing. I *do* smell."

And then the children held their noses and taunted her. "Uuuuurgh," they cried as they made a circle around her. "Pancake Face smells!"

At home that night, Alice's mother hugged her and told her that it was all right to have no nose. But Alice thought different. Every day people pointed and sniggered and looked at her in disgust, so it really wasn't all right.

Alice began to wear a hood so that she could hide. She wore grey too, so that she blended in with the walls and cobbles of the town. Under her hood and in her grey clothes, Alice slipped silently by, like the rats and mice. She flitted by, unnoticed like the sparrows.

At the end of every summer Alice would gaze up at the dark blue swallows gathering on the roof tops ready to migrate to Africa and the warmer places of the world where the sun shone all winter. She wished she could fly away with them.

Alice began to love the night, and the darkness that was kind and that would hide her.

She would look up at the stars and think that maybe there was a planet far away with people who *all* had no noses living on it – where to *have* a nose was a freak thing.

She knew that if she ever met someone with *two* noses she would never treat them like the people with noses treated her.

People hurt Alice's feelings all the time. As a result, she thought a lot about feelings and how they could be hurt.

—

Alice became a very compassionate person. She always tried to put herself in other people's shoes and understand what it was like to be them. This was one of the good things that came out of Alice's childhood.

# CHAPTER 3

# The Red Nose

One day, when Alice was twelve, she went to the circus with her mother and father. They sat in the front row. Alice pulled her hood low to hide her face.

The show started. There was a performing pony, a dancing bear, a tightrope walker and then there were clowns.

Georgia Byng

Three clowns rode unicycles round and round
the ring, throwing buckets of water at each other.
One of the clowns was really, really tiny – as small
as a four-year-old child.  The audience had come to
marvel and laugh at his smallness.

Alice watched him.  She didn't laugh.  Instead
she was caught up in thoughts about how brave
he was.  As the show went on, with the spotlight
on the ring, she relaxed in the dark and her hood
fell away.  But then the small clown tripped up and
tumbled towards her.  All the lights followed him
and the spotlight suddenly shone on her.  A big pool
of bright light drenched Alice.

The audience gasped, but not because the clown's trousers had come off showing his polka dot underpants. They gasped in amazement at Alice's moon face, with its two holes that were her nose. And then the laughter and the shouts came.

Being laughed at for what she looked like by so many people all at once was so horrible and so shocking that for a moment the world stood still for Alice. Wild laughter rang in her ears until it deafened her and she heard nothing.

When she dared to look up, Alice's eyes met the clown's. His eyes were warm and knowing and kind. He looked deep into Alice's eyes and saw her terror.

He smiled and tapped his nose, his big red clown's nose that was tied onto his face with elastic. He blinked and nodded, then whispered, "You should get one of these, my darlin'. It might help."

The next day Alice's mother took her to the doctor and Alice asked for a pretend nose.

It was an unusual request, but the doctor agreed to help. Alice's pretend nose was a triumph. It was made of china and was attached to the frame of a pair of spectacles. The nose rubbed on her flat face and made it sore, but Alice didn't care because when her disguise was on, at last she felt normal.

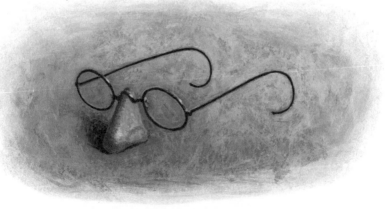

# CHAPTER 4

# Daisy

When Alice was sixteen, her parents died in a tram accident.

It was the start of a new life for Alice. She sold the family house and bought one in the city. She stopped wearing her hood, and instead wore a bonnet. The bonnet had a very large rim in case she still needed to hide, which she often did.

Alice started work as a typist in a solicitor's office. At her new job, no one knew that Alice had no nose. She chose a desk in a dark corner and kept herself to herself.

Alice was lonely. When the other girls ate their lunch together and gossiped, Alice would slip away up the narrow stairs that led out onto the roof garden. There she would feed the birds. They became her friends.

Eventually a human friend did turn up for Alice.

One spring morning, a girl called Daisy arrived. She sat near Alice. Daisy was very clever and knew hundreds of poems and stories by heart. After work, the two girls would sit by the fire and Daisy would

tell Alice stories.  Or Alice would help her with her

typing. Daisy loved words, but she often spelled them wrong, which would get her into trouble with the office manager.

One day, Alice was off work, ill with a cold, and Daisy made some terrible mistakes. She was typing a letter to one of the manager's clients.

"Dear Mr Bumsmell," Daisy typed. "I hop you are enjoying your horridays."

When he got the letter, Mr Bunsnell marched into the office, slamming doors behind him. Daisy was called up in front of the manager and sacked.

Afterwards Daisy wrote Alice a long letter that was full of spelling mistakes. But full of stories too.

Stories like the one about when Daisy had helped her friend by painting her market stall signs, but had spelled lots of the words wrong so that they read –

**'HEEL P EYE'**

instead of **'EEL PIE'** and

**'BANG HERS AND MESS AND BRISTLE SPRITES'**

instead of **'BANGERS AND MASH AND BRUSSEL**

**SPROUTS'.**

People gathered to laugh at the signs, but then they smelled the food. Daisy's friend did a roaring trade at the market that day.

"I diss eyeded to ignor my bad speling," Daisy wrote. "Becus I am so cleva in so menny other ways. And you, Alis, shood ignor your no-nose. Becus you are wunderful. You are the most wunderful, kynd person I hav ever met. I luv you and miss you. We will be frends for ever. Daisy."

After Daisy left the office, Alice retreated to the shadows again.

She watched the other secretaries from her dark corner desk and saw that they were the type of girls who cared more about what people looked like on the outside than what they were like inside. They were more impressed by what people had than what they did. The quiet girl in the corner was of

no interest to them.

One day Alice heard two of them complaining.

"Oh my nose is so big. I wish it was smaller."

To which the other replied, "But mine is so sharp. I wish it was rounder."

'They don't know how lucky they are,' Alice thought. She knew they would find her repulsive if they saw her without her no-nose disguise. 'If I were very rich,' she thought, 'if I lived in a very grand house with scores of servants, would they want to be friends with me then?'

'Perhaps yes,' she thought, but Alice knew that all the money in the world could never buy her a dear friend like Daisy.

# CHAPTER 5

# Monsters

Daisy had whetted Alice's appetite for stories. Without Daisy to tell hers, Alice found books with stories in them that she could read to herself. She found many stories with characters who were missing a part of their bodies.

In *Treasure Island*, Alice met Long John Silver, the notorious pirate who hopped along on a crutch with a parrot on his shoulder.

In *Moby-Dick*, there was Captain Ahab, who also had a false leg. It was made of whale bone. His real leg had been bitten off by the giant whale, Moby Dick.

The saddest story Alice found was the one about Quasimodo, the deaf hunchback who lived in the tower of Notre-Dame cathedral in Paris, where he rang the bells. He had a huge hump on his back and a massive wart that covered his eye and a bulbous face. The townspeople feared him as a sort of monster. But he wasn't. Underneath his hump and his lumps, he was a sweet person.

Alice also encountered Frankenstein, a creature built by Dr Frankenstein. The doctor built

Frankenstein using body parts gathered from the dead people of hospitals and cemeteries that he then sewed together.  So Frankenstein looked like a sort of patchwork person.  Wherever he went, he was shunned.  Loneliness and hatred drove him mad and turned him bad.

Alice found that lots of stories had villains that were odd-looking.  Witches had big, crooked noses and hairy warts all over their faces.  Trolls had twisted, heavy features.  The Cyclops only had one eye.

Alice started to understand why people found *her* repulsive.  In stories, anyone who didn't look

quite right, who wasn't a perfect human being, was destined to play the evil part or to be the monster. Alice realised that perhaps she reminded people of a monster, of some horrid thing from a story or a nightmare. And so she frightened them. She scared people who didn't stop to think that she was actually human and that it must be very difficult being her.

Alice read and read, but she couldn't find any stories where the *heroes* had missing parts or looked different.

She found some heroes who were *lame* – like Tiny Tim in *A Christmas Carol*, who got about on crutches and who thawed Scrooge's frozen heart. Or the boy in the *Pied Piper of Hamlin* who was too crippled to keep up as the other children followed the Piper into the hills and was left behind, the only child in the town.

In *The Steadfast Tin Soldier*, Alice finally found a hero who had a part of himself missing. The tin soldier had only one leg. He loved a paper ballerina so much that – after falling from a window, after being set adrift in a boat, after sailing along gutters, after floating into the sewers and out to sea, after being eaten by a fish – he at last made his way back to her.  The fish that had eaten him was caught and served up in the nursery where the ballerina stood on the mantelpiece.  But, disgusted by the one-legged tin soldier, a nasty child threw him into the fire.  The ballerina was blown into it too, by the wind.

And so the tin soldier and the ballerina were both burned.  Only ashes remained, plus a lump of tin that was the tin soldier's heart and, beside it, a tiny spangle of the ballerina's.

Alice sighed.  She saw that no one wanted heroes or heroines with missing parts – missing noses or ears, and with no arms or no legs. Alice thought of beggar children she had seen with hare lips, their mouths pulled and bent crooked, and she knew that no stories would tell of a hero or heroine who looked like that. These children were seen as monsters. Just as Alice was. And monsters couldn't be heroes. Or could they?

One day Alice used her understanding of other people's narrow minds and their fear of monsters to her advantage. This is how.

## CHAPTER 6

# Brushes and Sticks

For all the time that Alice had worked at the solicitor's office, an old chimney sweep had worked the street, with a little boy to help him.

Alice would watch the boy trot along behind the old man, carrying all the brushes and sticks needed for cleaning the sooty London chimneys.

The boy's master was a cruel man. Every now and then he would turn and swear at the boy and cuff him hard – even in the open street with people looking. Alice knew the boy must get much worse beatings behind closed doors.

He reminded Alice of the black mice she'd seen running along the railway tracks.

Alice hated to look out of the office window to see the young sweep's anxious glances as he dodged his master's fists.  The whites of the boy's huge eyes looked extra white in his face blackened with soot.  He was dressed in dirty rags.  Alice saw how thin he was and how often he coughed.  She supposed the chimney sweep liked to starve him so that he wouldn't grow, so he stayed small.  That way he could be stuffed up chimneys more easily.

One October afternoon Alice met the chimney sweep boy.

It was the time of year when winter was fast approaching and there was a flurry of chimney cleaning in the city. The office manager had called the sweep in to talk about cleaning the building's four tall redbrick chimneys.

Alice watched from her corner desk, unseen in the shadows, as they talked. The master sweep grovelled and bowed to the office manager until he was given the job.

But as soon as the office manager went downstairs, he stopped pretending to be nice and a cruel look darkened his face.

"Today I want you up there like a shot. You hear me?" he chided the boy. "An' don't you come down, laddie, until I says so. You're a lazy little tyke. I'll light a fire up your flippin' backside if you don't move swift ... D'you hear me, you little beggar. Fancy a flamin' backside?"

He snarled at the boy, then punched his shoulder and walloped him over the head with the back of his hand.

"Now get up there," he barked, thrusting a big brush at him, "and don't even think of snivellin' or cryin' to anyone or I'll shop you to the coppers an' say you've been stealin', and they'll 'ang you for that."

"But I never ..." the boy objected.

"Shut up an' get goin'."

Alice watched with horror as he pushed the

boy up the chimney and then, once he'd gone, took

a huge slug from a bottle of whisky or some other

brown brew he kept in his pocket. As he drank, he chuckled to himself. "I'll light 'im up. He'll shoot up that chimney like a firework."

The dastard man started to pile kindling in the hearth. Then he patted his pockets for matches.

Alice took her chance to slip past him and make her way up onto the roof. She put her no-nose contraption in her pocket and hitched up her long dress. She needed to scramble over a roof wall, up some slippery slates and then climb to the chimney pots.

It was difficult, but at last she found the chimneys connected to the fireplace in her office.

And, sure enough, she very soon heard frightened shouts coming from inside it.

"Please don't!" the sweep's boy was crying in a muffled voice. "Please, Mister Jim, put it out. I'm cleanin' them as fast as I'm able!"

A ragged wisp of smoke started to rise from the chimney and Alice could hear the boy coughing very close to where she was.

"NOOO! DON'T, MISTER JIM. I can't breathe!"

Quickly she loosened and removed the chimney stack. A cloud of black smoke hit her in the face.

Down in the chimney was the boy, blinking and spluttering up at the light. Beneath him, Alice could hear the cruel, drunken laughter of Mr Jim. Alice

reached for the boy and helped him up and out. He

was light as ash.

Alice led the boy to her rooftop chair, then rushed downstairs to get him some water and a currant bun left over from her lunch. She hurried back and gave them to him.

"Here you are," she said, out of breath. "What's your name?"

"Benjamin. Ben for short. Thank you, Miss," he said. "You're so kind. If others was more like you, Miss, there wouldn't be so much troubles in this world."

He looked up at her, his face beaming with sweetness and gratitude. Alice realised that her no-nose contraption was still in her pocket. She wasn't a monster to this boy.

It was then that an idea hit her – one where her monster face would come in very useful.

# CHAPTER 7

# The Fire Spirit

A few days later, Alice did something very cunning.

Late one foggy night, when the streets were deserted and the gas lights were dim, Ben let Alice into the basement of the master sweep's house. The brutish man was upstairs, half drunk and talking to himself.

Beside the fireplace, Alice found a scullery bucket full of cold ash.

She rubbed some of the ash onto her face. Then she swung her grey velvet cloak around herself.

She tiptoed up to the master sweep's room. She peered round the door. There he was, sitting with his eyes shut, in an old, worn armchair.

Alice spoke, but in a thin, half-whispering, smoky voice. "Mister Jim, Mister Jim!"

The sweep looked about, his nervous eyes peering into the gloom. "Who's that?"

"It's me, Mister Jim, the spirit of the fireplace."

"What? What you talkin' about?" Mr Jim clutched the arms of his chair.

Alice, peeping through the crack in the door, saw that the time was right to put the real frighteners on the sweep.

Georgia Byng

She let the door creak open so that the
flickering light from the fire lit her up.
She was a vision of horror to Mr Jim.

There Alice stood, draped in grey, her face white, her two eyes bright but blackened around the edges where she had darkened them with coal. Her mouth was coal black too. And her nose? She didn't have one.

Mr Jim took a sharp intake of breath. "What ... who ... what ...?" he garbled.

"Mister Jim," Alice whispered in her phantom voice, trying to sound as ghostly as possible. "All the fire spirits of London are angry. Angry with *yooooooooooou*. Your cruelty has disturbed the dead from the city's graveyards *toooooooo*."

Alice paused.

Mr Jim had turned so pale and clammy-looking that Alice thought he might be about to have a heart attack.

"Uuuuuughhhhh …" He let out a petrified grunt.

Alice went on. "The fire spirits have seen how you treat your sweep boys. And the fire spirits are angry. You are cruel beyond words to the boys who work for *yooooooooou*. We have seen. We are watching. Watching *yoooooooou*. And, Mister Jim?"

"Errrgh … erm … ergh, yeees?" Mr Jim gasped and stuttered.

"From now on, we warn *yoooou*, you *must* treat your sweeps well – feed them properly, dress them warmly and don't ever raise your hand to them again or we, the fire spirits, will haunt you every night. We will put a fire up behind you and burn this house to the ground *with you in it!*"

Alice left Mr Jim shaking in his chair. She shrank out of the room and slipped downstairs.

"I think you'll be all right now," she whispered to Ben as she left.

He smiled at her. "You're the best, Miss Alice."

"Night, Ben. Sleep well." She gave him a kiss. "Life will be a bit better for you from now on."

And it was.

Ben became like an adopted son to Alice. He still swept the chimneys, but Alice's warning saw to it that Mr Jim treated him like royalty. He gave him sausages for breakfast, hot pies at midday and tasty stews for his tea, and he never cuffed him, hit him or swore at him again. He certainly never lit any fires underneath Ben as he climbed up the chimneys. Mr Jim was a changed man.

But life wasn't better for everyone.

Sometimes Alice would lean her elbows on the wall of the office roof garden and look down at the city streets, busy below. She would see people whose lives were harder than hers or hard in different ways.

There was the little match girl, thin as a stick herself, who sold boxes of matches on a corner near

the tram stop.  Alice often bought a box or two from
her and gave her pocket money for food.

There was the tall, dark-skinned man who had
a lovely face.  Alice had heard that he was from
Africa, a place where very few people in London
were from in those days.  Alice had seen people spit
at him and call him names just because his skin
wasn't white.

One Saturday Alice went into the office to
collect a book she had forgotten.  She could hear
shouts and jeers.  She looked out of the window to
see crowds gathering around the jib that stood at
Horseferry Road.  Three men were being led up the

steps to the platform where the noose hung and the hangman waited.

Alice turned away. Even though she knew the men were criminals she still felt pity for them. She thought how terrified they must be, knowing their lives would end in a few short moments, knowing their necks were about to be broken. Yet Alice knew that the baying crowd cared nothing at all for their feelings.

When Alice sat down on her rooftop bench, she heard the crowd cheer and she knew that the three men were dead. A cloud hid the sun and for a moment the world seemed like a very dark place.

# CHAPTER 8

# Bright as a Shiny Penny

Alice saw that the world was often a cruel place –
somewhere with sinister things and bad people in it.
But there were good bright people in the world too.
And some of them changed Alice's life for the better.

One such was the tanner boy.

Like the chimney sweep's boy, the tanner boy
had a peculiar job, one that children in London don't
do any more. His job was to walk about the city and

pick up any animal poo he could find, put it in his sack and, at the end of the day, take it back to his family's tannery.

A tannery was where leather was made and tanners were the people who made it. It was a good job to have, but a very smelly one. And here comes a warning. If you are queasy perhaps you shouldn't read this next bit.

A tanning workshop always stank – as did the houses where the tanner families lived – because the only way to take the hair and fat off a dead cow skin, and so make soft, hairless leather, was to soak it in a pool of animal wee and poo. This mixture is so acidic that it melts the fat and hair off the animal skin.  This is why the tanner children walked around the city looking for the ingredients for the revolting tanner 'soup'.

When the 'soup' had done its job, tanner men had to take the sloppy animal hides out of the stinking slop pool, scrape off the hair and fat, then rinse the skin to get the sordid smell off it.  By the time the skin was cleaned and oiled and ready to sell, it didn't smell bad at all.

But tanner people always had a bit of a whiff about them, and so they kept themselves to themselves.  Only tanner girls could put up with the smell of tanner boys, which is why tanner men always married tanner women.

And nobody from outside a tanner family ever wanted to make friends with a tanner. The boy with the brown sack, whom Alice saw collecting poo off the street, was a boy no one ever talked to. Alice decided that she would talk to him, and so, one day after work, she waited for him.

At five o'clock he came along. His eyes were glued to the pavement and gutters, a little shovel was in his hand.

Alice stood beside a pile of horse droppings, knowing he would stop by it. Sure enough he did. She watched as he scooped the stuff up and plopped it into his sack.

"Good evening," Alice said. "I expect you are going home soon, as your sack is very full."

The boy gave her a puzzled look and shied slightly, as if expecting her to spit at him. Then, seeing Alice's smile, he tipped his cap.

"I'd like to buy some leather," Alice went on. "Can you take me to the tannery?"

The boy nodded. "Certainly, ma'am. Follow me." He was quiet for a moment, then he added, 'I'm Charlie by the way."

"I'm Alice." Alice held out her hand.

Charlie shuffled in his hobnail boots, and then he examined his own filthy hand. He wiped it on his black shorts and held it up to her.

'He really is dirty,' Alice thought, 'in his brown stained jacket and shirt that might once have been white.' But she took his hand and shook it.

Georgia Byng

Charlie didn't smell bad to Alice. She couldn't smell him at all.

As they walked to the tannery, they talked.

Charlie's nature was as bright as a shiny penny.

He spent hours on the streets every day and saw people coming and going, though no one saw him, except to avoid him. He knew the history of the city and its stories, about the people who had lived there long ago, as well as fresh stories that were only a day old.

"There are good things about smelling bad," he told Alice. "I am invisible in lots of people's eyes and so I see things that other people don't. And

although I am less than a person to most people,
I meet the kindest people in the world as only the
kindest people talk to me." He smiled at Alice and
nodded in approval at her.

When Charlie and Alice arrived at the tannery
where the leather workshops were, Charlie's mother
was locking up the shop that faced out onto the
street. She was a rosy-faced woman with smile lines
etched around her eyes. Alice looked at them and
saw that she'd had a lifetime of smiling. She invited
Alice into her shop.

Alice picked up a red leather box from the shelf.
She took her glasses off – and so her pretend nose

too – and put her no-nose contraption into the box. It fitted perfectly.

"Could have been tailor made for it," Charlie's mum said.

Alice nodded. She was bare-faced but she felt safe. "I've been looking for a new case," she said.

Alice bought the red box and was shown around the tannery. She met Charlie's dad, his grandmother and his uncle and cousins. Alice knew that the place probably reeked like a sewer, or like the rotten old fish that had been held under her no-nose as a child, but she couldn't smell anything. And she discovered that, contrary to what people said, the tanning people were very clean when they were not working. After work, bathtubs were filled in a back room for everyone to wash in. Each child was scrubbed clean.

"You can see how clean we are," Charlie's mother said. "The pity is that the tannery smell clings to our clothes and our hair no matter how hard we scrub."

As they ate supper together, Charlie told Alice how he and his cousins didn't go to school. The local school didn't want them.

"I have an idea," Alice said. "I could come in to see you on Saturdays and teach you how to read.

There are so many stories I could read you. When you open the reading door all sorts of ideas and facts and stories come tumbling through it." She paused, suddenly uncertain. "Unless you like to go to the hangings on Saturdays?"

Charlie's mum shook her head. "We would never do that, sweetheart. And you are always welcome here. And we would be most grateful if you was to open that reading door for us."

And so Alice taught the tanner children to read. And the tanners became Alice's friends. She wondered whether the tannery smell lingered on her clothes, but no one ever complained even if it did.

She loved being at the tannery and she loved the freedom of not wearing her no-nose contraption. Warmed by the love of her new friends, Alice found that she didn't care if she did smell. After all, no one in the office wanted anything to do with her anyway.

# CHAPTER 9

# Lovely in the Sun

Five years passed ...

One day a handsome man with a sunny nature came to work in the office. He was called Mr Coram.

The office girls blushed and giggled when they were near him, and when he wasn't there they talked about frocks and the latest hairstyles. Every day the office was filled with new laughter and it grew more and more colourful as the girls wore new dresses with ribbons and shawls to match.

Mr Coram was like the sun making flowers bloom.  But Alice felt like a bog plant that would never bloom.

She didn't want Mr Coram to see her pretend nose and so she kept to the shadows.  When the office girls gathered around him, Alice would escape to the safety of her roof garden.  The roses she had planted were heavy with blossom.  She wondered what roses smelled like.

Alice grew unhappy.  Who would ever love a Pancake Face?  She had the birds, she had Daisy, and Ben, and she had her tanner friends.  But Alice wanted someone to share her life with, someone like Mr Coram.  In fact, Mr Coram.

Charlie, who saw everything that happened on the streets, had seen Mr Coram coming and going from the office, and he had seen, too, how much his friend Alice loved him.  He also saw how sad she was.

One day a parcel arrived for Mr Coram.  Alice watched as he opened it.  Inside was a small round leather box.  It was red – the same as Alice's red leather box, where she kept her no-nose contraption. There was a letter inside too.  Mr Coram read the letter, and he smiled.

He looked up to see Alice watching him. And he smiled at her.

The next day, Alice was on the roof enjoying the warm summer evening. Her glasses, and so her pretend nose, were on the bench beside her.

"Hello there, Alice," a kind voice said. Mr Coram walked across the roof garden towards her. Alice reached for her glasses but she knocked them. To her horror, her no-nose disguise clattered to the ground.

"It's lovely in the sun, isn't it?" Mr Coram said as he sat on the seat across from Alice.

"Lovely!" Alice said. "Atishoooo!" She pretended to sneeze and held a hankie to her face.

Mr Coram took out his own handkerchief and rubbed his eye.

Then Alice's mouth fell open and the hankie dropped from her face. Mr Coram had pulled his eye out of its socket!

"People used to call me Cyclops," Mr Coram said. His one eye twinkled. "What did they call you, Alice?"

"They called me P ... P ... Pancake Face," Alice stuttered.

Mr Coram grinned. He polished his glass eyeball, took the small red leather box out of his pocket and put the false eye away in it.

Alice gazed at the box and she realised that her dear friend Charlie had sent it to Mr Coram. For he, Charlie who saw things other people didn't, knew all about Mr Coram's missing eye.

Mr Coram leaned towards the ground and picked up Alice's no-nose disguise. He saw her

red leather box on the bench, and he took it.  He
opened it, slipped her spectacles and nose inside and
snapped the catch shut.

Then he took hold of Alice's hand and they sat
in the evening sun and talked.

# CHAPTER 10

# You Are a Bacon

A year later, Alice and Mr Coram began a toy company. They called it "False Faces for Fun".

And what about Alice and Mr Coram's own false faces?

They never wore them again.

And what about Daisy? She became a writer of stories.

And the tanner family and Charlie?  They read, among other things, the stories that Daisy wrote.

And Ben?  Well, Alice and Mr Coram adopted him.  He was the page boy at their wedding.  He never went up another chimney again.  Alice brought him out of the shadows and into the light.

Alice lit up the path for lots of people.  And they in turn illuminated her life.

"You are a bacon," Daisy wrote.  "A lite horse, a torch, a landturn, a son, a bolb, a mutch, a ray."

*Be a beacon. Be a lighthouse, a torch, a lantern, a sun, a bulb, a match, a ray. Be anything that lights the right way.*

# About *The Girl with No Nose*

This book was inspired by an item at the Hunterian Museum in London. A false nose mounted on the bridge of a silver spectacles frame, with straps to hold the spectacles and nose in place. The nose itself is hollow, painted to match the patient's flesh. A doctor gave the item to a woman who, a few years later, returned with the nose in her hand. She said that her new husband liked her better without the false nose than with it.

So, when I wrote Alice's story, I was thinking about the woman with her false nose. I was also

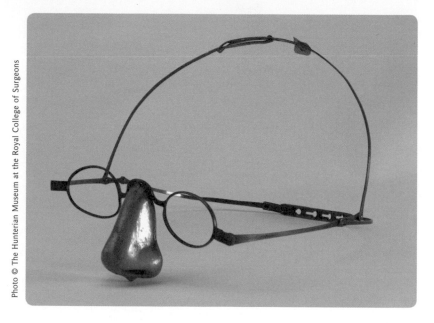

thinking about the ancient Japanese idea of

wabi-sabi.  If only Alice had known about it!

Wabi-sabi is the idea that there is wisdom and

beauty in that which is imperfect.  No one is perfect.

We are all imperfect.  And our world is, of course,

massively imperfect. Alice is incomplete without her nose, but that does not stop her from becoming a brilliant person.

I love the way that a real person with no nose – a woman who lived more than 150 years ago, who never knew that she was going to inspire a story – has helped create this book. And I hope that this woman's real life, one where she came to terms with her no-nose-ness, will inspire the people who read *The Girl with No Nose* to be proud of who they are, no matter what their imperfections are.

*Georgia Byng*